D1093806

Published by
Princeton Architectural Press
70 West 36th Street
New York, NY 10018
www.papress.com

Printed and bound in China
25 24 23 22   4 3 2 1 First Edition

ISBN: 978-1-64896-183-0

Published by arrangement with Debbie Bibo Agency

Book design by Orith Kolodny

This book was illustrated with watercolors, gouache, and
colored pencils.

For Princeton Architectural Press:
Editors: Rob Shaeffer and Parker Menzimer
Typesetting: Natalie Snodgrass

Library of Congress Control Number: 2022932471

What's the Rush?

Yiting Lee

Princeton Architectural Press · New York

It's a perfect afternoon.
A lovely day for tea with a good friend.

Turtle looks at the faraway
mountain and says,
"How beautiful! One day
I want to climb it."

"Once I'm ready," he adds.

Bunny has heard this many times before.

So Bunny says, "Let's go tomorrow!"

"Tomorrow? What's the rush?" asks Turtle,
before accepting Bunny's challenge.

The next morning Bunny
gets up early and goes over
to Turtle's house.

Knock knock!

But Turtle isn't ready.
"Hang on just one minute,"
he says.

"One more minute."

"Just another minute."

"*La la la...*"

"One more minute!"

What is Turtle doing?

"Hang on just one more minute,"
says Turtle.

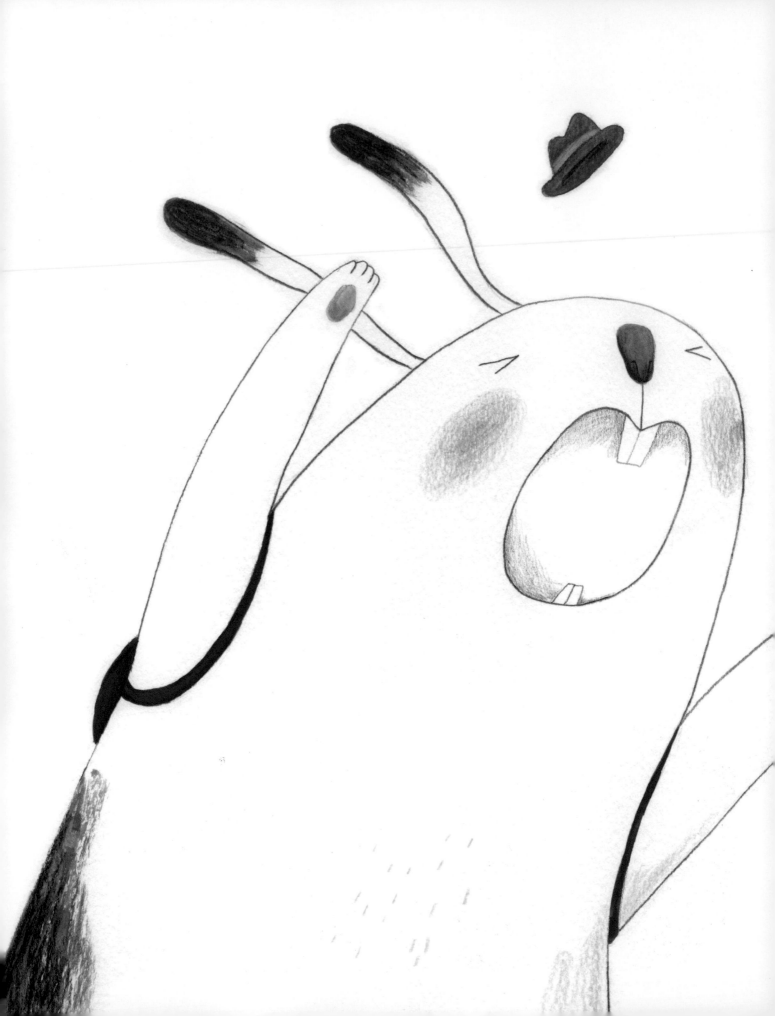

"No more
minutes!"

cries Bunny.

"What's the rush? I only needed a few minutes," says Turtle.

"Finally! Off we go!" says Bunny.

"Oh no," says Bunny.
"A river. How are we going to cross it?"

"Hang on just one minute," says Turtle,
and he pulls a raft out of his backpack.

"Oh no," says Bunny.
"Which way are we supposed to go?"

"Hang on just one minute," says Turtle,
and he opens a handy map.

"Oh no," says Bunny. "How can we get through these bushes?"

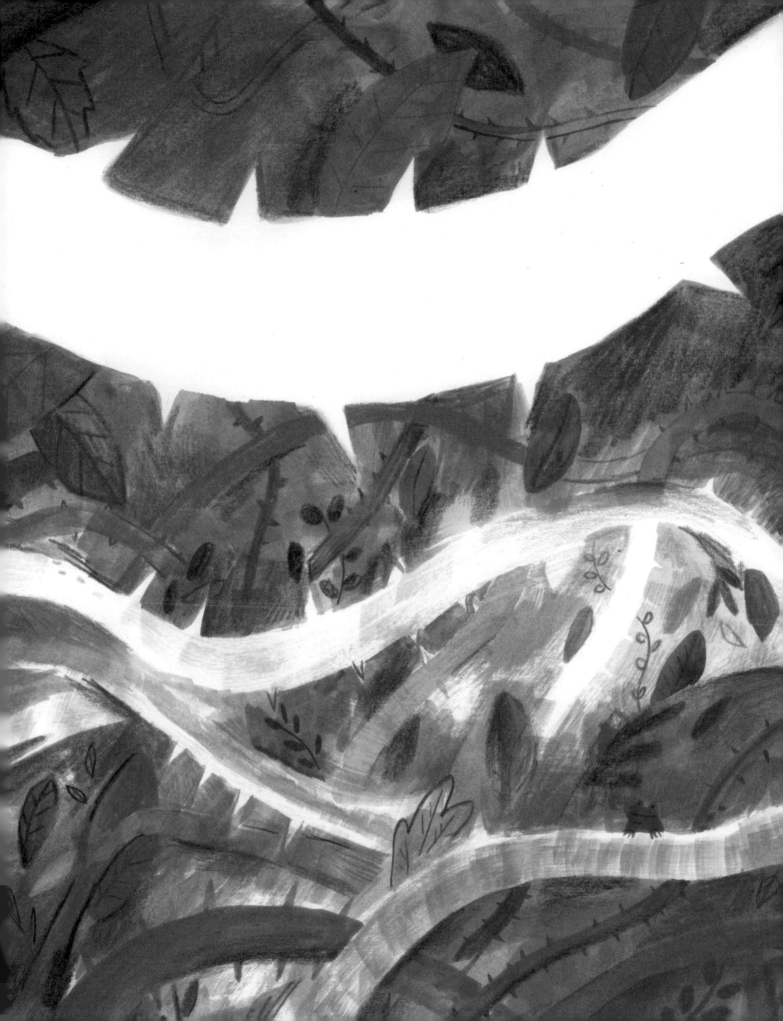

"Hang on just one minute,"
says Turtle, and he picks a tool from his
backpack to help clear the way.

They walk and talk and laugh.
Finally, they arrive at the top of the mountain.

"Hooray!" they both shout.

Then Bunny's tummy begins to growl...

"Hang on just one minute," says Turtle.
"Maybe this will stop your tummy
from grumbling."

The moon rises and owls begin to hoot.

Turtle looks at the moon and says,
"How beautiful! One day I want to go there."

"How about tomorrow?" says Bunny.

"What's the rush?" asks Turtle.

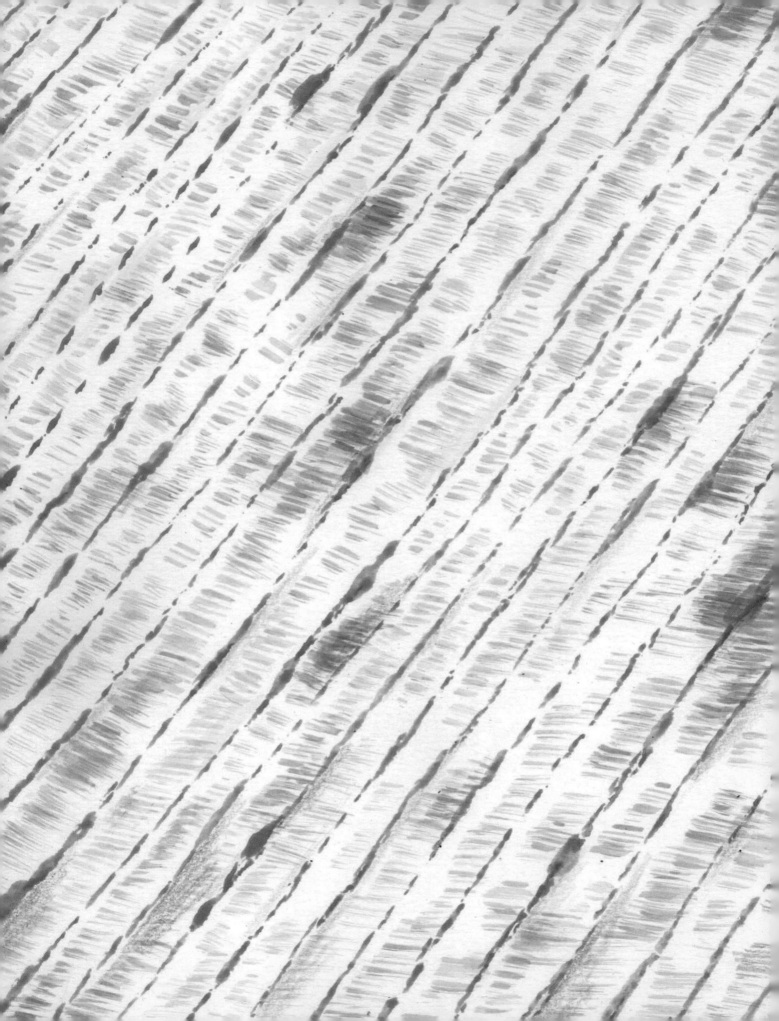